Aidan's First Full Moon Circle

Written and Illustrated by W. Lyon Martin

WITHDRAWN

Help find my acorns!

A Magical Child Story

Magical Child Books
an imprint of Shades of White
Crystal City, MO
www.paganchildrensbookpublishing.info

For my husband, TC.

Aidan's First Full Moon Circle

The illustrations were created in watercolor, gouache and pencil on 140lb Kilimanjaro cold press. Text was set in Berliner Grotesk.

Publisher's Cataloging-in-Publication Data

Martin, W. Lyon
    Aidan's first full moon circle / Written and illustrated by W. Lyon Martin
    p. cm.
    ISBN 978-0-9796834-4-2
    Summary: Aidan and his parents, solitary witches, are invited to a local coven's Full Moon Esbat celebration. Aidan participates during the ritual by casting the Circle.

[1. Neopaganism--Fiction. 2. Holidays--Fiction. 3. Wiccans--Fiction. 4. Wicca--Fiction. 5. Goddess religion--Fiction. 5. Rites and Ceremonies--Fiction. 6. Ritual--Fiction.] I. Title.

PZ7.L9883 AID 2008
[E]--dc22   2007904404

Printed in the United States by Corporate Graphics Commercial, North Mankato, MN 56003

"Hi! I'm Seamus. I'm collecting lots of acorns to get me through the long, cold winter. You can help me.

Every place I appear in the story, I have a pile of acorns. Count how many I have then find the same number of acorns in the picture to my side. Can you find all the acorns?"

Aidan's eyes popped open. He was too old for naps, too excited for sleeping. His family was Circling with a coven tonight. They celebrated holidays home alone most of the time. Wasn't it time to leave yet?

The coven was camping at a place of Earth Power. Aidan strained to hear the potent Power's humming. Tree branches mimicked hands reaching for the sky. Aidan wondered what a Circle in the woods would be like. He fretted about new people he'd meet.

Everyone met for a potluck dinner. Afterwards, a bonfire was lit. Wood crackled as it burned. The breeze blew smoke at Aidan's face. A nice man handed Aidan a little drum so he could play with the other drummers. A steady beat vibrated his body. Soon, the Moon rose. Hair on the back of Aidan's neck prickled. He stopped drumming. Behind the drummers Mama and High Priestess watched him. Had Aidan done something wrong?

High Priestess approached Aidan. She looked down at him and smiled. "Yes, I think you'll do fine." She handed him a long staff. "Will you cast our Magick Circle tonight?" she asked.

Aidan gulped. What an honor to be asked to cast Circle! All he could do was grab the staff and nod.

When he finished Aidan and Papa stepped into an opening left for them. The group turned north, east, south, then west, welcoming each direction's Element into Circle. High Priestess glanced around. She tilted her smiling face toward the Moon. She began chanting and swaying. The gathered coven followed her lead.

They gathered around the glowing embers. High Priestess asked volunteers to call the four directions.

"Want me to walk with you?" whispered Papa. Aidan breathed in deeply, "Yes." He'd be braver with Papa nearby.

High Priestess raised her arms into the sky. She called in a loud voice, "Tonight, we celebrate the Harvest Moon!" Then she nodded at Aidan. His throat tightened as he moved forward.

Aidan's hands shook as he lifted the staff high. Carefully parading clockwise around the Circle, he called. "I cast this Circle between the Worlds!" He continued to strut around the Circle. "I create a sacred place!" He paced the Circle three times. He repeated the words Papa used during family rituals.

Aidan chanted and swayed. He began sweating. He threw off his jacket. All around the Circle, cloaks fell to the ground. Clouds drifted away from the Moon. A moonbeam struck High Priestess' face. She glowed. Aidan saw himself glowing also.

Steam rose off the chanting people. Their ritual gathered lots of energy. The chanting swelled to a roar. The swaying people rocked faster and faster.

Suddenly, High Priestess yelled, "RELEASE!"

Everyone in the Circle shouted, too.

Aidan tingled from the energy's release. Papa and Mama placed their hands on the ground. So did Aidan. Everyone touched the ground. The group faced each direction to thank the Elements for joining them.

Aidan strolled outside the Circle chanting, "The Circle is open, but never broken. Our ritual is done!" Three times around he journeyed. He didn't need Papa's help this time.

Aidan yawned. He dragged himself to their tent and crawled in. He watched the Moonlight disappear as the clouds closed over the opening. His eyelids drooped. Raindrops pattered on the tent. He fell asleep.

Aidan woke early. He poked his head out the tent flap. He stole quietly outside. His breath puffed in front of his face in the chilly air.

Aidan explored a stream nearby.

Aidan splashed his face.
Across the stream stood
a deer with her fawn. She
looked him in the eye.
Aidan reached out a
hand and froze.

"Good morning, Sister
Deer," he whispered.

Icy water dripped down
his collar. He closed his
eyes and shivered.